The Red Slippers

and other princess stories

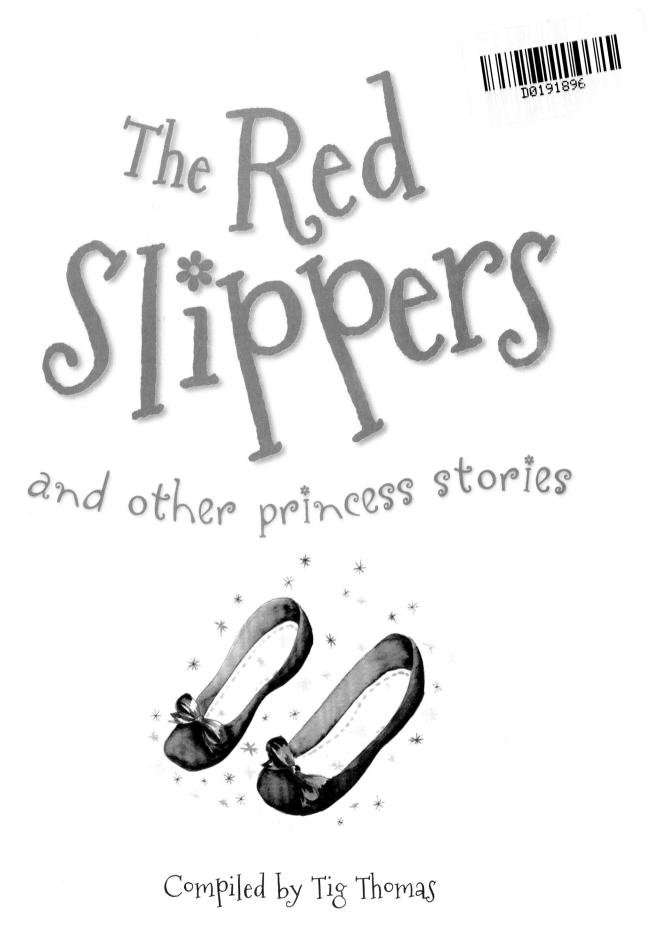

Compiled by Tig Thomas

Miles
Kelly

First published in 2013 by Miles Kelly Publishing Ltd
Harding's Barn, Bardfield End Green, Thaxted, Essex, CM6 3PX, UK

2 4 6 8 10 9 7 5 3 1

Publishing Director Belinda Gallagher
Creative Director Jo Cowan
Editorial Director Rosie McGuire
Senior Editor Claire Philip
Senior Designer Joe Jones
Production Manager Elizabeth Collins
Reprographics Stephan Davis, Jennifer Hunt, Thom Allaway

ISBN 978-1-78209-218-6

Printed in China

British Library Cataloguing-in-Publication Data
A catalogue record for this book is available from the British Library

ACKNOWLEDGEMENTS
The publishers would like to thank the following artists who have contributed to this book:
Smiljana Coh, Kirsten Wilson, Jennie Poh, Karen Sapp (cover)
All other artwork from the Miles Kelly Artwork Bank

The publishers would like to thank the following sources for the use of their photographs:
Cover frame: Karina Bakalyan/Shutterstock.com
Inside frame: asmjp/Shutterstock.com

Made with paper from a sustainable forest
www.mileskelly.net   info@mileskelly.net

Contents

The House in the Wood

A POOR WOODCUTTER once lived with his wife and three daughters in a little hut on the borders of an enormous forest.

One morning as he was going to his work, he said to his wife, "Let our eldest daughter bring me my lunch into the wood, and so that she shall not lose her way, I will take a bag of millet with me, and sprinkle the seed on the path."

When the sun had risen high, the girl set

out with a basin of soup. But the birds had picked up the millet long ago, and the girl could not find her way.

She travelled until the sun set, then she saw in the distance a light, so she began walking towards it.

The girl knocked at the door of a small house, and a gruff voice called, "Come in."

When she opened the door there sat an old, grey-haired man at a table. His face was resting on his hands, and his white beard flowed all over the table.

By the stove lay three animals – a hen, a cockerel and a

brindled cow. The girl needed a place to sleep, so she asked for a night's lodging. The old man with the long, grey beard said,

"Pretty cockerel,

Pretty hen,

And you, pretty brindled cow,

What do you say now?"

"Duks," answered the beasts, and that must have meant, "We are quite willing," for the old man went on, "You are welcome, go into the kitchen and cook us a supper."

The girl found plenty of everything in the kitchen and cooked a good meal, but she did not think of the animals.

She placed the full dishes on the table and sat down opposite the grey-haired man. When she had eaten her fill, she said, "But now I am so tired, where is a bed in which I can sleep?"

Then the old man said, "Go upstairs, and there you will find a bedroom."

The maiden went upstairs, and when she had made the bed, she lay down. After some time a trapdoor beneath the bed opened, and she fell down into the cellar.

The woodcutter arrived home late that evening, and he scolded his wife for leaving him all day without food.

"The girl went off with your dinner," she answered. "She must have lost her way, trying to find you."

At daybreak the woodcutter set off for work, and this time asked his second daughter to bring his food.

"I will take a bag of lentils," he said, "they are larger than millet, and the girl will be sure to find her way."

At midday the maiden set out with the

food, but the lentils had all gone. She wandered on, until she came to the old man's house, and asked for food and a night's lodging.

Again the man with the grey hair again asked the animals if she could stay. The animals answered, "Duks," and everything happened just as before.

The girl cooked a good meal, ate and drank with the old man, but did not trouble herself about the animals. And when she was asleep, the trapdoor opened once more. She slid down into the cellar, where she found her sister.

On the third morning the woodcutter said to his wife, "Send our youngest child today with my dinner. She is good and obedient, and will keep to the right path. I will take plenty of peas with me and strew them along, they are even larger than lentils, and will show her the way."

But when the maiden started off with the basket on her arm, the wood pigeons had eaten up the peas, and she did not know which way to go. At last, when it grew dark, she saw the little light, and came to the house in the wood. She asked prettily if she might stay there for the night. The man with the white beard asked his animals the question again. The animals said, "Duks."

After she prepared a good supper for herself and the old man, she said, "We have had plenty while the good beasts have nothing. I will attend to them first."

Then she went out and fetched barley for the cockerel and hen, and brought the cow sweet-smelling hay.

The maiden then went upstairs, made the

bed and fell asleep. She slept peacefully until midnight, when there was such a noise in the house that she awoke.

Everything trembled and shook, the beams swayed and the roof fell in with a crash. Then all became still, and as no harm came to the maiden she lay down again and fell fast asleep.

But when she awoke in broad daylight, what a sight met her eyes! She was lying in a splendid room, the walls were covered with golden flowers, the bed was of ivory and the counterpane of velvet.

The maiden thought she must be dreaming, but the door opened and in came a handsome young man, who said, "I am a prince, and was condemned by a wicked witch to live as an old man in this wood with my three servants, who were transformed into a cockerel, a hen and a cow. The spell could only be broken by the arrival of a maiden who should be kind not only to men but to animals. You are that maiden, and last night at midnight we were freed. My house was transformed into my palace. Will you become my princess?"

The girl joyfully accepted, and as they

stood there the prince told his three servants to go and fetch the maiden's parents to be present at the wedding feast.

"But where are my two sisters?" the youngest daughter asked.

"They are in the cellar," he said, "Let us go and set them free, and see if they will join us on our wedding day."

The Red Slippers

By Gertrude Landa

ROSY-RED WAS A SWEET LITTLE GIRL, with beautiful blue eyes, soft pink cheeks and glorious red hair. Her mother died the day she was born, but her grandmother looked after her. She was very happy. All day long she sang, and so lovely was her voice that birds gathered on the trees to listen to her.

On her first birthday, her father's gift to her was a pair of red leather slippers. Now, although neither she nor her father knew it, they were magic slippers, which grew larger as her feet grew. Rosy-red was only a child and so did not know that slippers don't usually grow.

One day, Rosy-red returned from the woods to find her grandmother gone and three strange women in the house. "Who are you?" she asked.

"I am your new mother," answered the eldest of the three, "and these are my daughters, your two new sisters."

Her father appeared then and spoke kindly, telling her he had married again, because he was lonely and that her stepmother and stepsisters would be good to her. But Rosy-red hastened away to her own little room and hid her slippers of which she was very proud.

"If they have turned my dear granny out they will take my beautiful slippers from me," she sobbed.

After that, Rosy-red sang no more. She was made to collect firewood for the fire and draw water from the well. She struggled with the heavy bucket, the weight of which made her arms and her back ache with pain.

Sometimes her cruel and selfish stepsisters pushed her around. Often they went out to parties and she had to act as their maid. Rosy-red was only happy when her stepsisters were out of the house. Only then did she sing softly to herself, and the birds came to listen to her sweet, gentle voice.

So the years passed away and Rosy-red grew into a beautiful young woman. Once, when her father was away from home, her stepsisters went to a wedding dance. They told her not to forget to draw water from the well, and warned her that if she forgot they would be horrible to her when they returned home.

So Rosy-red went out in the darkness to draw water. She lowered the bucket, but the cord broke and the pail fell to the bottom of the well. She ran back home for a long stick with a hook at the end, and as she put it into the water she sang sweetly, "Swing and sweep until all does cling, and to the surface safely bring."

It so happened that a sleeping genie dwelt at the bottom of the well. He could only be awakened by a spell, and although Rosy-red did not know it, these words were the spell.

The genie awoke, and he was so pleased with the sweet voice that he fastened the bucket to the stick and put some beautiful jewels inside.

"Oh, how beautiful," cried Rosy-red when she saw the glittering gems. "I will give these jewels to my sisters. Perhaps then they will be kinder to me."

She waited until the sisters returned from

the dance and showed them the jewels. They were too dazed to speak when they saw the sparkling precious stones. Then they asked how she came by them. Rosy-red told them of the words she had sung.

"Ah, we thought so," said the sisters, sneakily, to her horror. "The jewels are ours. We hid them in the well for safety."

They told her to hurry off to bed, then snatching the bucket they hurried off to the well. They lowered the bucket and sang the words. At least they thought they sang, but their voices were harsh. The sleeping genie awoke again, but he did not like their croaking voices.

"I will teach you to disturb my sleep with hideous noises," he said. "Here are some more croakers," and he filled the bucket with slimy toads and frogs.

The Red Slippers

The sisters were so angry that they ran back home and dragged Rosy-red from her bed. "You cheat," they exclaimed. "Get out of the house at once!"

Rosy-red had only time to snatch her pretty red slippers and put them on. On and on she walked, much further into the woods than ever before. The magic slippers guided her, and as darkness fell she noticed a light a short distance away.

When she got quite close, Rosy-red saw that the light came from a cave. As she neared the entrance an old woman came out to meet her. It was her grandmother, but Rosy-red did not recognize her at first. Granny, however, knew her straight away. "Come in, my child, and take shelter from the rain," she said kindly.

The inside of the cave was surprisingly

quite cosy, and Rosy-red, who was completely exhausted, quickly fell asleep. A few hours later, she awoke with a start.

"Where are my red slippers," she cried.

She put her hand in the pocket of her tattered dress, but could only find one.

"I must have lost the other," she sobbed. "I must go out and look for it."

"No, no," said Granny. "You cannot do that. A storm is raging."

Rosy-red sobbed herself to sleep, but was woken up again by voices. She crept into a corner of the cave and listened.

A man was speaking. "Do you know who this red slipper belongs to?" he was asking. "I found it in the woods."

Rosy-red was moving forwards when she heard her granny say, "No, no, I don't know." The man left.

Granny came back into the cave and said, "I'm sorry, but he might be a messenger from your sisters, and they only wish you harm. We don't know if we can trust him."

The next day, the man called again, this time with several servants. Again, Rosy-red concealed herself.

"I am a prince," said the man, "and I must meet the wearer of this shoe. Only a graceful and beautiful girl can wear such a dainty slipper."

Day after day he came, each time with more servants. Finally, he came with one hundred and one servants.

"The girl I seek is here," he said. "Deny it no longer. My servants heard a young girl singing here yesterday."

Rosy-red trusted the man's voice, so she stepped out bravely, wearing her one red slipper. The stranger, bowing before her, held out the other slipper, and placed it on her foot. It fitted her perfectly.

"Many girls have tried to put on that shoe," said the young man, "but all have failed. Let us get to know each other, and if you like me I have sworn to make you my bride. I am a prince, and you shall be a princess."

So Rosy-red left the cave with her granny, and was led through the woods to her new home where she knew only happiness. And she always wore her magic red slippers.

Spindle, Shuttle and Needle

By the Brothers Grimm

Many people used to make thread from cotton using a spindle. They would weave the thread into cloth using a loom and a shuttle. A needle was then used to sew the cloth.

THERE WAS ONCE A GIRL whose mother and father died while she was still a little child. Her godmother lived all alone in a small house and earned money by spinning, weaving and sewing. The old woman took the child to live with her and taught her all she knew.

When the girl was fifteen years old, the old woman became ill. She called the child to her bedside, and said, "Dear girl, I feel my end drawing near. I leave you the little house, which will protect you from wind and weather, and my spindle, shuttle and needle, with which you can earn a living." Then she laid her hands on the girl's head, blessed her, and said, "Keep the love in your heart, and all will go well with you." Then she closed her eyes, and soon after she died.

The girl lived alone in the little house. She worked hard, spinning, weaving and sewing, and the blessing of the good old woman was on all that she did. It seemed as if the flax in the room increased of its own accord, and whenever she wove a piece of cloth or carpet, or made a shirt, she at once found a buyer. She had just enough money to buy what she needed.

About this time, the son of the king was looking for a bride. He was not allowed choose a poor one, but did not want to have a rich one. So he said, "I shall make a girl my wife if I can find one who is the poorest, and at the same time the richest."

When he came to the girl's village he asked, as he did wherever he went, who was the richest and also the poorest girl in the place? The people in the village first named the richest. The poorest, they then said, was the girl who lived in the small house.

The rich girl was sitting in all her splendour before the door of her house, and when the prince approached her, she made him a low curtsey. He looked at her, said nothing, and rode on.

When the prince came to the house of the

poor girl, she was sitting in her little room. He stopped his horse and saw through the window, through which the sun was shining, the girl sitting at her spinning wheel. The girl looked up, and when she saw that the prince was looking in, she blushed and went on spinning.

She carried
on until the king's
son had ridden away,
then she went to the
window and looked
after him. When she
could see him no
longer she sat back
down to work again.

A saying that the old
woman had often
repeated came into her
mind, and she sang these words outloud
to herself, "Spindle, my spindle, haste,
haste you away. And here to my house
bring my husband, I pray."

And what do you think happened?

The spindle sprang right out of her hand
in an instant, and out of the door, and

when, in her astonishment, she got up and looked after it, she saw that it was dancing merrily into the open countryside, and drawing a shining golden thread after it.

Before long, the spindle had entirely vanished from the girl's sight. As she now had no spindle, the girl took the weaver's shuttle in her hand, sat down to her loom, and began to weave instead.

The spindle, however, danced onwards, and just as the thread came to an end, it reached the prince.

"What do I see here?" he cried, "the spindle wants to show me something!"

So the prince turned his horse

29

around, and rode back, following the golden thread. Meanwhile, the girl was sitting at her work singing, "Shuttle, my shuttle, weave well this day, and guide my husband to me, I pray."

Immediately the shuttle sprang out of her hand and out by the door. Before the threshold, however, it began to weave a carpet that was more beautiful than anyone had ever seen. Lilies and roses blossomed on both sides of it, and on a golden ground in the centre, hares and rabbits, stags and deer bounded, while brightly coloured birds sat in the branches above. The shuttle leapt here and there, and everything seemed to grow on its own accord.

As the shuttle had run away, the girl sat down to sew. She held the needle in her hand and sang, "Needle, my needle, sharp, pointed and fine, prepare for a husband this house of mine."

Then the needle leapt out of her fingers, and flew everywhere about the room as quick as lightning. It was just as if invisible spirits were working. The needle covered tables and benches with a beautiful green cloth in an instant, and the chairs with velvet, and hung the windows with pretty silk curtains.

The needle had just put in the last stitch when the maiden saw the white feathers of the prince's hat through the window, The spindle had brought him there by the golden thread. He got off his horse, stepped over the carpet and walked into the house. When he entered the room, there stood the maiden in her poor garments, but she shone out from them like a rose surrounded by leaves.

"You are the poorest and also the richest," he said to her. "Come with me, if you like, and you shall be my bride."

She did not speak, but she gave him her hand. Then the prince gave her a kiss, lifted her on to his horse, and took her to the royal castle.

A great wedding took place soon after. The spindle, shuttle and needle were kept in the treasure chamber, and held in great honour.

Odds and Ends

A German fairy tale

Flax is a natural material collected from
the flax plant, which can be spun into
fine thread and used to make linen.

THERE WAS ONCE UPON A TIME a
maiden, called Gretel, who was
very pretty, but lazy and careless.
Her mother had taught her to spin, but
Gretel could not be bothered to take care
with her work.

When she had to spin, she got so angry
and impatient that if ever there was a little

knot or tangle in the flax, she wouldn't work carefully at it to smooth it out. Instead, she would simply pull the knot out, and a whole heap of the flax would come with it. Then she would toss it down onto the floor. By the time Gretel had finished spinning, the floor around her would be covered with lumps of flax, good flax that need not have been wasted if only she would take the trouble to carefully tease out the knot.

Now, the family had a servant named Griselda, who was as patient and hardworking as Gretel was lazy and careless. She baked the bread, brewed the beer, fed the cat, milked the cow, made the cheese, and kept the house as clean and neat as a pin.

Each evening Griselda swept the floor and

Odds and Ends

collected all the bits of flax Gretel had thrown down. Every night after her work was done, she would sit by the fire in the kitchen and tease out the knots and clean the flax. Then she would spin it into fine thread. From that thread she wove a beautiful piece of cloth, which she dyed cornflower blue. She then made a beautiful gown for herself. She didn't have many chances to wear it, as she worked so hard.

One day the prince of the land stopped at Gretel's house for a drink after he had been out hunting. Griselda prepared a tray of cakes and poured a mug of beer. As she went to carry out the tray Gretel took it.

"Don't worry about that," she said, "I'll give it to the prince." And she did, and looked lovely in her apple-green dress, with her blue eyes and red-gold hair. The prince thought he had never seen a prettier girl, so he invited Gretel to go riding with him that day, and the day after − and every day after that he came to see her.

One day he told her that his father was holding a ball and begged her to come as his special guest. Of course Gretel said yes, and flew home to tell her mother and father the happy news. What a bother there was as they worked to get ready the beautiful dress, the shawl, the fine shoes and jewels that she would need. Of course Griselda did all the work, and Gretel sat by the fire warming her toes and giving instructions.

When the night of the party drew near, Gretel kept poor Griselda busy, making her wash, then curl her hair, and fix her dress to perfection. At the last minute Griselda slipped into her cornflower dress, and without any other preparation walked behind the carriage to the ball.

Gretel was the belle of the ball, and for the first half the prince danced only with her. Griselda danced merrily with anyone who asked her. After one dance, glancing at her over her shoulder, Gretel said to the prince, "Ah, look at that girl, dressed in my odds and ends."

The prince asked Gretel what she meant, so she explained to him that Griselda was wearing a dress made of the flax that she had thrown away.

When the prince heard how lazy Gretel could be, and how hardworking Griselda was, he chose Griselda as his wife instead.

So Griselda married the prince and went to live in the palace. She was always very happy and busy, helping the prince rule the kingdom, caring for the poor and running the palace. Gretel married a forester and had to learn to work a little harder, which did her good.